Mrs. Lancevich

FARMER GROVER

by Norman Stiles

illustrated by
Tom Cooke

featuring
Jim Henson's
Muppets

SESAME STREET BOOK

blished by Western Publishing Company, Inc. in njunction with Children's Television Workshop. 1977 Children's Television Workshop. Grover 1971, 1977 Muppets, Inc. All rights reserved. inted in U.S.A.